Babar characters TM & © 1990 L. de Brunhoff
All rights reserved.
Based on the animated series "Babar"
A Nelvana-Ellipse Presentation
a Nelvana Production in Association with The Clifford Ross Company, Ltd

Based on characters created
by Jean and Laurent de Brunhoff

Image adaptation by Van Gool-Lefevre-Loiseaux
Produced by Twin Books U.K. Ltd, London

This 1990 edition published by JellyBean Press,
distributed by Outlet Book Company, Inc.,
A Random House Company, 225 Park Avenue South,
New York, New York 10003

ISBN 0-517-05210-5

8 7 6 5 4 3 2 1
Printed in Italy

BABAR™

and His Friends

At Home

Twin Books

JellyBean Press
New York

What a lot is going on outside the palace today!

Arthur is trying the  he just got.

"Look, Flora," he calls, "how fast I'm going!"

But Flora isn't paying attention to Arthur. She

is playing with a new  .

Pom and Alexander are playing basketball with

Zephir's .

"Look at that! I made a basket!" cries Alexander,

throwing the ball onto the  !

Behind a  , the Old Lady is talking

with Celeste about the garden.

roller skates, jump rope,
ball, balcony,
hedge

"I must smooth the path in the garden," says

Pom, picking up the big  .

"You are full of energy," the Old Lady tells him,

putting on her  to keep off the sun.

"Instead, please get the  . It's been

days since we had even a drop of rain here in

the garden. The  is all yellow."

Celeste and Flora are picking flowers to make up

a pretty  for the Old Lady.

"Look, Mama," says Flora. "I have just found

the loveliest . I'm giving it to you."

rake, hat, watering can, lettuce, bouquet, rose

In the garage, Olur, the mechanic, is fixing

Babar's car. Alexander has climbed up onto

a 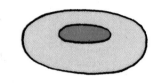 to get a close look at all the

inner parts of the  as Olur works.

"See, this piece is worn out," explains Olur.

Zephir is pretending he is a mechanic, too.

He offers Olur a blue  for the motor.

"Oh, no," laughs Arthur. "He can't use that.

It's for pumping a 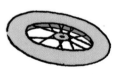 that's gone flat.

I know what Olur needs," he proclaims proudly,

holding up the big  .

tire, engine,
bicycle pump,
bicycle tire,
pliers

Suddenly, in the darkening sky, a huge rain

 appears. A strong gust of wind

rattles the red  on the house.

Flora and the Old Lady have already gone inside.

Olur picks up his 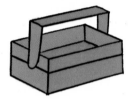 and says,

"I'm going home before the storm starts. Bye!"

Pom runs to put away his work

in the garden shed. Alexander and Arthur

are shutting up the 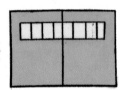 of the garage.

"Come along," calls Celeste to the children.

"It's raining. Come into the  ."

cloud, shutters,
tool box, boots,
doors, house

Beside the  in the playroom,

Flora stands and watches the falling rain.

"Look!  ! Did you see it, Arthur?"

Arthur has missed it, because he is busy

looking for a game in the big  .

"Come see, Alexander!" calls Zephir loudly.

"There's a good Western on the  set!"

"Chug, chug, chug," says Alexander. "I'm playing

with the  . Whoo, whoo!"

"Please, quiet down a bit!" complains Pom. "I'm

trying to put this big jigsaw  together."

window, lightning, toy box, television, train, puzzle

s downstairs to welcome

...king wet! "What a

...got to take along my

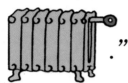 this morning."

Come and get warm," says the Old Lady. "You can

stand by the ."

"Look, Papa, I've brought your 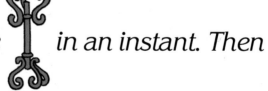," says

Flora, jumping into Babar's arms, wet as he is.

Zephir climbs up onto the in an instant. Then

he reaches out with a grin and deftly takes off the

wet ⬡ on Babar's head.

umbrella, radiator,
slippers,
coat rack, hat

Babar has gone into his study to work.

Seated in his grand office , he looks at

a  from his library. "Papa, don't

you want to play with us?" asks Flora. She is

tugging his  with her trunk.

"I'm sorry, children, I must work," replies Babar.

"Please don't disturb me at my 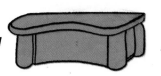 ."

But little Alexander doesn't want to go. He is busy

punching the buttons on the  . Now

Babar's patience with the children is growing

short. "Go play with Arthur," he tells them.

chair, desk,
book, telephone
jacket,

The children are playing a game of hide-and-seek.

"Ninety-eight, 99, 100!" calls Alexander, who is It.

Running up the 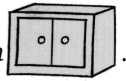, he looks for Arthur, Pom,

and Flora, who are hiding in a  .

They are trying hard not to make any noise, but

they are crowded by the . And Pom

and Flora can't keep from laughing at poor Arthur,

who is all tangled up in the  !

"Ouch! I'm getting squeezed," whispers Arthur.

Hanging from a  , Zephir is laughing

at Alexander as he looks for the others.

stairs, cupboard,
stepladder,
vacuum cleaner,
chandelier

Babar and Celeste hear a crash. "Look!

The big purple  has fallen off the cupboard!"

But where are the children? they wonder. Then

Arthur knocks his head against a  ,

and a  falls over with a loud clatter.

"We were just playing hide-and-seek," he explains.

"Why don't you play in the attic," suggests Celeste,

giving them the  to the attic door.

Zephir comes running down the stairs with

the  so that Arthur can press his

wrinkled clothes.

vase, hanger,
broom, key,
iron

The children climb up to the attic, where

Pom opens a big wicker  and finds

one of his favorite old toys. He cries, "Wow!

My  ! I thought it was lost!"

Zephir is watching a that is busy

spinning its web. He would like to catch it.

Suddenly, Flora climbs onto a

and calls, "Look over there! Be careful! I see a

gray ! Help, help!"

Alexander thinks this is very funny. "I'm not

afraid of a mouse!" he boasts.

basket, clown, spider, trunk, mouse

Flora has dressed up in some old clothes,

with a magnificent pearl  and

fine made of lace. She thinks

she looks beautiful. Pom is wearing a general's

uniform. High on a pedestal, Zephir pretends

he's a statue. A with curls is on his

head. Alexander is riding the  .

"Booooo," moans a scary voice from out of the

darkness. Pom shrieks, "Help, it's a  !"

He jumps up quickly, and falls right into the trunk!

"Ha, ha! It's only me–Arthur!"

necklace, gloves,
wig, rocking horse,
ghost

After playing in the dusty attic all day, the

children are ready to take a bath.

Pom has turned on the tub  full

force, and the water is rising too fast to suit Flora.

She warns him, "Look out, the  will

run over on the  and get it wet." Now

what has become of the ? It's almost

impossible to find: it slips away in the water.

Under the , Zephir is singing at the top

of his voice. "Please stop!" cries Alexander. But

Zephir thinks his singing is lovely.

faucet, tub, bathmat, soap, shower

Now all the children are clean and dry.

Flora, wearing a  around herself,

is admiring the way it looks in front of

the 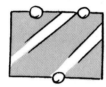 . Pom, his in hand, is

beginning to get impatient.

"Please, let me use the  ," he says. "It's

my turn, and you've looked at yourself enough."

Zephir has on a  and blue shorts.

Alexander is out of the shower and wrapped in

a  that is much too big for him–

because it belongs to Babar!

towel, mirror, toothbrush, sink, T-shirt, bathrobe

The children run down to the kitchen. Their

baths have given them an appetite. Luckily,

the is always full of food.

Pom picks up his and asks for milk.

"I would like to make a chocolate cake," says

Flora, "with that flour on the  ."

"Me too! Me too!" announces Pom eagerly.

"Very well," says the Old Lady, and she goes to

turn on the  for them at once. Flora

puts on a ruffled  to protect her dress

and says, "Let's get to work."

refrigerator, glass,
table, oven, apron

Standing on a stool, Flora breaks up a

large chunk of  . She is eating

more than she puts into the  !

Alexander is happily stirring the cake batter

in the mixing with a big spoon. "Watch

what you're doing," he advises Zephir, who

breaks the a little too hard.

Pom prepares a big for the batter.

"Well done, it will soon be ready to bake," says

Celeste. "When it's time, I'll take the cake out

of the oven."

chocolate,
saucepan,
bowl, egg,
cake pan

In the dining room, everyone sits down to

eat. The children are very excited. Zephir

even drops his  in his haste to finish.

"Now may we eat our dessert?" he demands.

Arthur can't wait: He has already taken

his  off his lap to go get the cake.

Flora is complaining, "Mama, I don't understand

why my  is blue and the others are red."

Alexander has rushed from the table to bring

out the tray of from the kitchen. "Look,"

he says, "I even remembered the  ."

*fork,
napkin,
knife,
cheese,
bread*

At last, the long-awaited moment is here.

Alexander and Flora carry in the  , all

covered with chocolate frosting and cherries, on

the heavy serving  of silver. "How

good it smells!" exclaims Celeste. Arthur is so

eager for the cake that he gets up to help put it

on the  . Then he cries, "Someone

has forgotten to give me a dessert  ! And

it must be a big one!" After everyone has said

"Congratulations" to the cooks, Pom says, "Let's

eat !" and waves his .

cake, tray,
sideboard, plate,
spoon

Everyone has eaten well, and they finish the

evening together in front of the warm 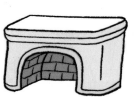 .

Flora asks her parents, "May I come and sit

on the  with you?"

The Old Lady is knitting a sweater for Babar.

"Where is my other ?" she asks.

"Oh, it fell down." Luckily, Zephir is holding

onto the big  , or she might have lost

that, too. "It's late," says Babar. "Time for bed."

Pom and Alexander, playing on the 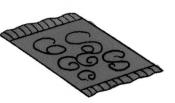 ,

would like to stay up just a little longer.

fireplace, sofa,
knitting needle,
ball of yarn,
rug

Zephir and Arthur are saying good night to the

little ones. Alexander has wound up the  .

It is really very late–past their bedtime.

Pom has put on his  , but instead of

going to sleep, he is jumping on his  .

Flora is wearing a  that has a pink

puppy pattern all over it. She always goes to

her  to say good night to her

fish. "Come along," says Celeste. "Time for bed."

She comes in to turn off the and gives

everyone a kiss.

clock, pajamas,
bed, nightgown,
chest of drawers,
lamp

Night has fallen, and the sky is clear. With

his in his arms, Pom sleeps.

Head under his soft , Alexander

dreams of chocolate cake. But Flora doesn't

feel tired even though it's so late.

"Don't close the , Mama," she begs.

"I want to look out at the bright crescent

and that . Aren't they beautiful?"

"Yes, they are lovely," Celeste agrees. "But now

you must get your rest. Good night."

Moments later, Flora, too, is fast asleep.

*teddy bear,
pillow, curtain,
moon, star*